T0374090

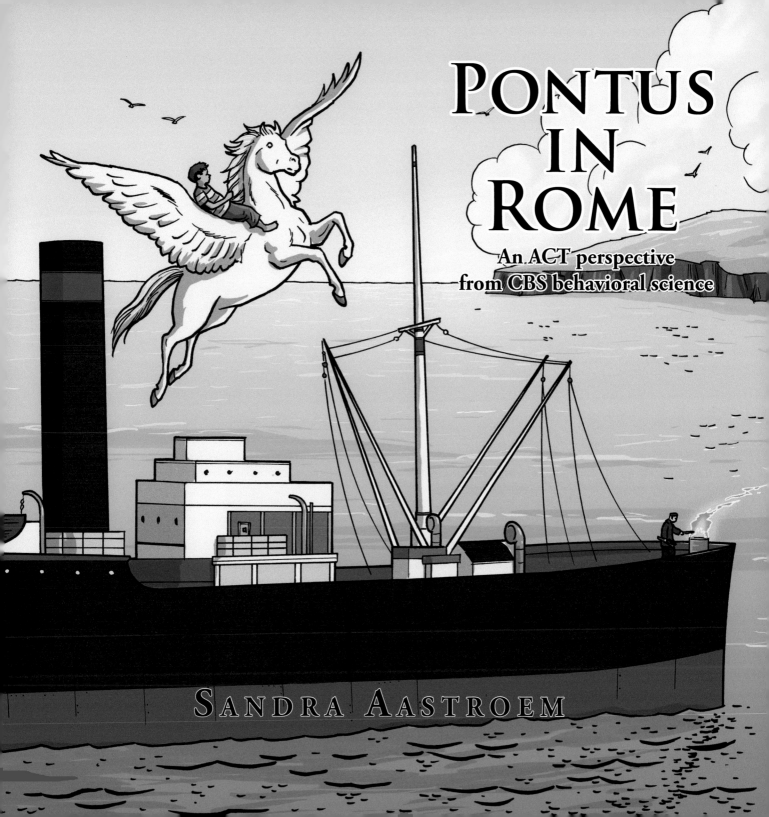

Pontus in Rome

An ACT perspective from CBS behavioral science

Sandra Aastroem

AuthorHouse™ UK
1663 Liberty Drive
Bloomington, IN 47403 USA
www.authorhouse.co.uk
Phone: 0800.197.4150

© 2016 Sandra Aastroem. All rights reserved.

No part of this book may be reproduced, stored in a retrieval system,
or transmitted by any means without the written permission of the author.

Published by AuthorHouse: 06/22/2018

ISBN: 978-1-5049-9620-4 (sc)
ISBN: 978-1-5049-9619-8 (e)

Print information available on the last page.

Any people depicted in stock imagery provided by Thinkstock are models,
and such images are being used for illustrative purposes only.
Certain stock imagery © Thinkstock.

This book is printed on acid-free paper.

Because of the dynamic nature of the Internet, any web addresses or links contained in this book may have changed
since publication and may no longer be valid. The views expressed in this work are solely those of the author and do not
necessarily reflect the views of the publisher, and the publisher hereby disclaims any responsibility for them.

authorHOUSE®

PONTUS IN ROME

An ACT perspective from CBS behavioral science

SANDRA AASTROEM

Pontus in Rome is a book about a boy named Pontus. Pontus is an 8 year old boy living in Rome, Italy. I want to say thank you to professor Masoud Kamali at Mid Sweden University and Uppsala University, for teaching me about the difficulties in understanding the complexity in cultures. Thank you also to the professors and teachers at the Mid Sweden University department of Social Work, for teaching me about understanding the methodology of science of Social Work. Thank you to my friends from the Social Worker education in Mid Sweden university. You always bring clarity and hope as well as strength to continue pursuing dreams and goals. The book is a descriptive interpretation of a Romany child´s migration with living in Rome. The book mirrors an ACT perspective from CBS behavioral science. I want to say thank you to Sverigehälsan AB, for teaching me about cognitive behavioral therapy and ACT. Thank you for listening and for being there as a guide with ideas and creativity. The history about Pontus guides the reader into seeing from an active child´s perspective, driven by and with focusing on the child´s thoughts, impulses, emotions, doings and behavior. Thank you also to My Family and friends who I love dearly. Thank you for all your help and support the last years. Thank you to everyone else who has helped generously in times of need.

For Vilmer Badman Aastroem and Maximilian Badman Aastroem

Always following your hearts with goals and dreams

Contents

ONE

Problems and Theories

Giuseppe Vicari writes in "Beyond conceptual Dualism" about the monism – dualism, body – mind dilemma and of the Desubstantialization of Mind. He sees the problem with the psychological and physical.

He mentions the work of Charles Darwin, Jean Piaget, Antonio Damasio, Gerald M. Edelman, Walter Freeman, Rodolfo Llinás and other scientists who suggest that we have to see our powers of knowledge, theoretical and practical reasoning, creativity, and so on – as tools that we use in fight for our survival, developed as extensions of our basic biological makeup.

"We can read these works as attempts to understand the embodiment of mind and consciousness as part of the evolutionary theory of biological organisms constantly negotiating their relationships with the environment, where the environment in question is physical and in the case of human beings social, institutional and cultural". (Beyond Conceptual Dualism; preface 2008)

Vicari discusses the work of John R Searle, one of the most authoritative voices in contemporary philosophy. The author is particularly concerned with the relations between mind and world. (on the nature of those relations) (Editorial foreword Beyond Conceptual Dualism; Editorial foreword 2008)

TWO

ACS AND CBS

Pontus in Rome is a book about a boy named Pontus. Pontus is an 8 year old boy living in Rome, Italy. The book is a descriptive interpretation of a Romany child´s migration with living in Rome. The book mirrors an ACT perspective from CBS behavioral science. The history about Pontus guides the reader into seeing from an active child´s perspective, driven by and with focusing on the child´s thoughts, impulses, emotions, doings and behavior.

The book focuses on the child´s perspective and has an important message of the Romany children living today in Europe where they stand with complex family needs in the society. The Romany culture is often associated with difficultness and the Romany is trying to find ones place in the European way of life. Pontus in Rome is an attempt to focus on the child´s perspective of this.

THREE

PONTUS IN ROME

Well. If you´re not inspired to write, from this paper background; - to write a fantasy tale. I was to write about something that I had experienced. I felt I had to write about something I had to tell. But would I manage to? That was the underlying question going around in my head the last days. The paper was full of flowers and it had a nice green background. It was really inspiring and it was fulfilling to feel how the pen was working on the paper.

It was easy writing, and uncomplicated it felt like. BACK to the question that was going around in my head repeatedly. After the divorce from Patrick everything was more complex in my life. There were many thoughts to gather threw and just going around in my head. I didn´t have any inspiration to write before, I remember by the way. I was in a squared way of thinking, stuck in my ordered way of thinking. It was important that everything was placed in its right place. It was important with efficiency in the daily life. The hats was sorted with the hats. The gloves was sorted with the gloves. The pony horses - from when I was a little girl growing up - with the pony horses and the adventure guys with the adventure guys. Systems with boxes. Everything in an efficient machinery.

In the office it was similar like in the rest of the house. When I think about it, the computer was the most structural item, remaining threw the changes. Now to the point. The computer gave no inspiration to writing. Maybe it gave better result to write when writing creative texts? Therefor I tried writing on this colored paper. From back in the time - when I was in school, I remember the pupils writing in the classrooms. There were no computers to help then. There were lined papers and special school pencils to write with. And I remember it was easy to write then.

Could I make it, thus was the underlying question, as I was making the pencil work on the paper. There was something I wanted to tell and put into words. A sense of warmth grew inside. It was anxiousness. Everything went along well so far and it felt good writing down the story. I gazed upon the paper and the details stood out like in 3 D. Would I manage to finishing what was to become a book?

I felt it was meaningful to write about something that I had experienced. The story was about Pontus, a Romany child who lived with his mother on the streets of Rome. This is the story about him, the boy in Rome.

The boy´s name was Pontus. Pontus had been given his name, - a European name from his mother "to fit into the European way of life". A name that was easy to pronounce would make it easier for him, meant his mother. Romany people are from India and the Romany people are a travelling people. "Romany people travel but to our family it is important to fit in" Pontus´s mother had said to him many times. It was difficult to fit in - for a child, in the dusty old streets of Rome. The streets are no good place to be living on for a child.

Imagine the streets for a place for a living for Pontus of seven years. There were a lot of things Pontus could manage, but there were a lot of danger also. On his bare children's feet he ran on the streets. He was seeking different jobs and a chance for a meal. It was dusty as he ran but it made no difference for he enjoyed it running there.

There I had started writing the story about Pontus! So far it went easy with writing. I find it interesting to see the child's perspective on his life. The story is actual and I remember how I had seen this little boy on a street in Rome. The flowers stood out from the paper and helped to imagining the story. It was almost like being there yourself.

Pontus reminded me about my own son, when I had my son with me there in Rome. The boy we saw in Rome was older and so independent. He was kind of a strong child, happily running around with his bare children's feet. There was an understanding that this child would manage to live through a lot. The child would grow up to be a man in spite of living on the streets. I wonder how the scenery with its street surroundings were in the winter time. Where did the boy live in the winter time? Did he have grown ups there, and was he safe? Did he have anyplace warm to live? He must have had someplace warm to live in the cold winter nights or was he much like no outside on the cold streets I wondered.

The street life for the little boy Pontus meant much in the day time, to be around the tourists in Rome. Pontus enjoyed being in the Piazzo Navone square. There were also many of Pontus´s friends around in the square. There was always an interesting conversation among the street performers and the artists. They spoke in a fast dialogue where it was to be fast spoken even for the children. For Pontus it meant that he rapidly grew into being a social, quick minded and curious boy who had many thoughts.

Pontus spent much time helping with different chores. This day it was market day on the square.

-"Pontus will you come on over here and will you please tell me about your week"! Alonso shouts and gathers some fruit from a fruit box.

Pontus watches this; – apples, oranges... and dreamingly he counts them.

-"Bring some more oranges? You think? Yes I think you´re right! 8, 9…. Well! How was your week boy? Did you go by the Trevi fountain, making any wishes? Here´s some coins, 50 cents, here you go boy. Make a wish and see if it can come true… " Alonso continues.

In some way there was always joy and a light way of seeing on life. Pontus never felt poor or missed any things. All that Pontus had and all that he was given he was given by his friends and mother on the street. Pontus feels happy and shines up when he answers Alonso:

-"Yes... Thank you"

He continues to sort amongst the fruits when Theresa shouts at him in French:

-"Do you understand me? Are we speaking the same language? Eh? Come!"

Pontus enjoys to kid around with Theresa. Theresa is a woman who doesn´t have any children of her own to take care of, in Italy. Her children are in her home country. There it is hot like the sun! Pontus enjoys Theresa's happy way and her warm personality. There is always something good in what she says and she has a good eye for Pontus. It can be different things, a helping hand, something good for lunch and so on. Pontus likes it. There are days when there aren´t any euros for food.

There comes Pontus´s mother walking towards him and she gives him a warm hug.

-"Hi little Pontus. Do you know how it came to be, that you were given your name, young man, she asks."

-"Yes…" Pontus answers for he knows this answer.

He has heard this story many times. It is the story about when the beautiful horses one day fly down through the sky, from their places on that museum house. It was a fascinating explanation that was inspired by both history and magic. Pontus´s mother enjoyed to tell this story about how it happened, when Pontus was given his name - but now there wasn´t any more time.

More and more people were coming to the market. On the marketplace of Piazzo Navone there now were romans and tourists "from different locations in Europe" as Pontus´s mother said to him many times. The market was flourishing and on the square there was growingly more and more sounds. The sounds were loud of happy people who on this market day, had come to make something nice to buy. You could be finding the ingredients for a dinner you were making for the siesta. Pontus also thought it could be nice, to buy some of the beautiful figurines of his friend Ronald or anything else. On the market there was something for everyone, knew Pontus. And romans love good markets. All people did - by the way, and Pontus´s friends worked and often had busy days to make the market work well. "Free from deficiencies" like Ronald points out, to the market people, as good as daily.

So they worked together making this meeting place pleasant for the guests, who were on the streets of Rome for different reasons. Pontus´s heart started to pound from excitement to the all more arisen market excitement. Like this it was for Pontus, when Pontus was at the market. This is a story based upon a true story. That is important.

My thoughts wander off to other issues. There is much to think about I feel and I feel tired, even though I've only been awake for some hours. I should be feeling rested. I think about the time when I was carefully sorting things into boxes. Now there are other things to think about.

The market was growing with people and the sounds where loud. People were talking, making bids and shouting in different languages. The market people were running in different directions, making different bids, selling and negotiating. Over there Pontus saw some bag being sold. There he saw that some earrings were being sold. It was Pontus´s mother that had made these earrings. She was very talented in this making thought Pontus. Pontus thought it was a shame that the mother hadn´t had the opportunity to put the earrings into the jewelry shops in the Rome city center. Everyone that knew the family thought so. But one day maybe luck would change Pontus dreamingly thought on his mother. ONE day Pontus´s mother might just achieve her big dream of being a popular and well known jewelry designer in Italy. Pontus was very proud of his mother and of her ability to make the most delicate, funny, round lines - out of straight metal. Pontus´s mother was given the opportunity to work in a local silver shed in Rome city center, against her taking care of chores of cleaning in the working place and tidying up after the work in the shed.

Pontus´s mother had a sister. It was Pontus´s mother´s sister that I had seen that day, when I saw Pontus running barefoot in the old city. It was on that day I had seen her sitting down begging. She was begging for money in the entrance to the old church. Pontus was helping too. On bare children's feet he ran amongst the tourists. The woman in the stair case by the old church was sitting down and leaning with her head. Her sun colored face was showing just a little when she met the eyes of people passing by. The clock was nine and the woman was sitting by the place and so it continued through the day. The boy was moving gently from person to person, kind of watching out for the people passing by as well as begging for their help. He had gentle kind brown boy eyes. The situation on the streets of Rome and in other Mediterranean cities were for the homeless, to sleep in the street or in best case the local city shelter. Pontus sometimes slept in the city shelter, when there was room left.

Pontus dreamt about having his own home, like other people in Rome. Pontus and his mother only lived partly in an apartment in Rome, together with Pontus's mothers friend, a man named Alex. Pontus didn't complain but he spent much time dreaming. Many of the dreams were about having an own home. A warm home where you didn't have to feel cold. He wouldn't have to worry about thefts or that someone dangerous would come.

Pontus was dreaming about this place and painted the place vividly in his dreams. Pontus had a lively imagination.

Pontus much liked when his mother told him the story, when he was given his name. It had to do with the big bewinged horses that were on the military museum building. The birdlike horses were standing on the roof of the building, in the middle of the city. The horses and big angel like wings. Pontus had his name given to him, with the help of these giant horses on a military building museum of Rome.

The telephone was ringing and I focused on that. When it comes to the horses with birds' wings, they guard the military museum in Rome city center and the roman fighter that was historically active in the founding of Rome. There is always a lit fire outside of the museum and is said to keep away the enemies of Rome.

Pontus felt his mother's love for him, when she told him the fascinating story. Could it be true? Pontus wondered. Pontus's mother was sometimes dramatic and she was good at telling a story that reached the listener well in his heart. Pontus was close to his mother. He was feeling so bad when she was hurt in any way. Like when the man Alex was acting angry. Pontus shivered when thinking about him being mean like that.

Pontus was watching his mother's face as she was working. In the sun light he could see her face being wrinkled in a special way, when she was smiling. She had long thick hair coming down her shoulders.

Pontus thought it was fascinating with the culture life in Rome. There were old sculptures being shaped thousands of years ago in a different period of time. By that time the painters and artists of the time were acting out their works putting their mark on today's architecture. Lupa Catolina Sanctura this day made Pontus imaginative. The Capitoline wolf was fascinating to a child. Everything was interpreted very strangely thought Pontus and watched the big wolf with her small wolf pups hanging heavily with their mouths, on her body. It was stone that had been shaped but it seemed real Pontus thought.

Pontus had heard the wolf cry out at night time when he was asleep, like a wolf from another part of the earth. Pontus was sure of that. It surely was crying out for its pups he thought. Pontus sometimes could imagine where the wolf belonged.

Pontus himself was from India. And where are wolfs from? The streets of Rome lie desert in the night time and it is raining when Pontus is walking outside tonight. Pontus is outside in the playground, where he likes to play sometimes. Pontus heads off for the climbing net that consists of a big round net area, heading for a tower. A slide runs down into a sand box where the children play. Pontus gazes over the playing area and his eyes stop on the volleyball court. He sees none of the big children that usually stay by the court. But then Pontus sees some of them sitting on a bench by the court wearing rain coats. The rain is smashing onto the ground when Pontus finds a playing tractor, in plastic to play with. He makes an intense humming sound, with his lips.

At Pontus´s mother´s working place in the silver shed she´s busy working on the silver. She has just ended her first working shift there and she now has the possibility to work on her jewelry. Sparks fly as she pounds on the steel with the hard club. She´s wearing ear plugs for protection against the loud sound. The environment is loud but the ear plugs work well.

Pontus felt it was great fun to play in the playground where he was playing with the tractor. The rain was falling into the sand making a sound. Drip drop. Drip drop. -SPLASH and a BANG. Pontus looks up, what was that? Were there someone else on the playground, except for Pontus and the bigger children? Someone bigger. Another BANG! Now a following series of claps coming and Pontus sees the horse and its carriage coming towards him making a clapping into the sand. The children are running away from it in different directions.

"-Did that come from the SKY?"

Clapiticlapiticlap. The horse makes a loud shriek and a quick turn in the sand with the wagon when it lands with its wagon and all.

-"It lives – It´s the horse from the national museum"! Pontus shouts out loud. "The horse is made of stone rock cement but it lives!"

 The shapes of the horse are crafted in hard material difficult for the strongest man to work on. Pontus sees the horse´s nice soft wings that follow the horses back and at once he grabs the horses black hair. He takes one step and a HOP! The feeling is intense when Pontus hops up on the horse´s back and the horse sets off running, and continues with lifting up from the ground flying into the rainy sky. A dripitidrop of heavy drops of water fall on Pontus and the big gestalt flew over the sky in a way that only happen in fairy tales or in imagination.

His dream had come true! It was a dream to be able to fly with the horse from the national museum. It was a true story that his mother had told him before. Had the mother seen the same horse? Pontus wondered. Were the horse now heading towards the national museum he continued. They flew over the houses roofs rapidly.

What was that? Pontus´s mother wondered as she saw some item in the sky heading by over the house roofs. She was walking home from the silver shed. It was raining and there was a cold wind grabbing her where she walked. She saw some item in the sky right above the Pantheon temple roof.

-"Ah. How cold and what cold weather" she said to herself.

She put her hair under the hood jacket that she was wearing. What was that flying there over the Pantheon roof? The rain had stopped her from seeing the item fully. She felt over her face and pushed the rain drops that where there away. She blinked rapidly and then the item on the sky was gone. It was windy and she was feeling cold from walking in the rain. She thought of Pontus and had he returned from the playground yet.

The horse and boy flew in the sky, above the house roofs. The boy grabbed the horse´s neck. The horse neck was warm and big. His hair from the head was hanging down the horse neck. They flew for a long time and Pontus thought of his friends on the Piazzo Navone square. His mother trusted them in taking care of Pontus and Pontus felt safe.

Away from the city and out to the country side they flew, over the trees and crops marks.

They flew out toward the sea and Pontus could see glimmering lights on the dark water. Clapiticlapiticlap! The sound was when the horse´s feet landed. What was THAT? They were walking on some firm land now, but it was moving in some way. It wasn´t the same clear claps as before thought Pontus. It was on a boat that they had landed. It was a shipping boat. Pontus looked up. The boat had a high crane on it for loading. Some seagulls where following the boat making dark shadows over the boats load.

How would the journey continue? Were the boat heading to another place, another country? Pontus wondered.

Pontus was feeling cold. He had been outside for a long time by now and he was tired. Pontus took a hold on the horse´s neck and slipped down the horse´s back.

Pontus felt sleepy and there was a spinning sense in his head. The boat was steaming thru the water but there was no possibility to see the water, because of the black night sky.

Pontus walked towards a door opening in to the boat. From inside the boat there was coming nice smells of spices. There were chopped onions on a kitchen bench. By the onion there was some kind of meat. The chef was hammering with something on the meat. There were sounds from pots with something warm inside, making bubbles come up and it ran up over under the lids. A man who was whistling joyfully on a tune was sitting next to the pots.

The fire place was making a nice sound from the wood burning under the stove and made it warm next to the stove. What would the chef say about Pontus and a big horse as a boat passenger outside? Pontus closed the door quickly and without a sound he had taken a bag of nuts with him from inside, for him and the horse.

-"Coo!"

The horse went a bit reflectively towards him, where he was holding up some of the nuts. The horse had a taste of the nuts from Pontus´s hand. Pontus was taken by a warm joyful feeling coming when he felt the horse´s warm mouth over his boy hand.

-"There!

Then Pontus ate some nuts himself. Pontus was eager to see what kind of boat this was and what was underneath in the boats shipping area. With rapid gentle steps Pontus went off and he found a door that led down to a stairway beneath. Sparkling fire met Pontus as he came down the foot of the stair case. There was a controlled fire coming from a big fire place and he saw the sight of charcoal. There was a bearded man standing working on the fire, Pontus noticed.

A load with blue cars was on the opposite side of the boat. Pontus laid himself down on the floor. Then he couldn´t remember anything more.

He must have fallen asleep for quite some time and when he was awakened he felt a numbing ache from the back, where he was lying on the hard floor. Pontus had to walk out carefully, so that nobody would notice that he had been there. He went the same way back. As he walked outside he pulled his sweater hard around his body and felt the cold a bit less. The horse was standing where he had been standing before and Pontus pushed himself up the horses back, for in the next moment, feeling the horses clapping feet set pace on the floor and then they lifted into the cold night sky.

Oh what an adventure this was! This was a dream to fly with the horse from the museum. From what the story had told him, the horse was able to fly and it did.

This is the story of a child with difficult living conditions and it shows Pontus's life as sometimes being hard. Pontus dreams a lot and wonders what life would be like for him and his mother, with different living conditions. He dreams about cars that you can play with from children's stores. Sometimes Pontus's mother had given him a euro that she had been given. Even so Pontus couldn't buy toys. Instead he bought something else - some good cockey or something other - to eat. When Pontus was given money from begging, he used to buy things from the market. He liked ice cream but that was a rare treat to those who were poor and partly living or more on the street. Pontus did and therefore he spent his money on what he needed. It was often last minute for buying clothes for there were no money and nobody had asked Pontus about practicing sports like it was possible for other children to practice sports.

What now. Are there coffee stains on the colored writing paper? Imagination sets off when I see the colored paper.

Oh, how nice it was to travel through the sky! Pontus and the big horse flew and the little boy looked out over the light shimmering city. The lights from cars where gleaming up the city. The boy was watching down over the city of Rome. When Rome was built it was dominated by strong cultures. During the empire of emperor Augustus there where many conquests being made. The city had its provinces far away from the boarders of Rome, towards Asia to the East.

Alexander the great took on the Turkish city Ephesus.

The Pergamesian king took over the city, when the romans gave the rule to the Syrian king Antrochos. for enabling the city to once again being ruled by the romans, on king Atollos' death bead. Before then the city was under Greek Athens protection and supported Sparta during the Peloponnesian wars.

King Mithridades started leading the Anatolian cities into rioting the Roman rule. Emperor Augustus then ruled.

More about the city of Ephesus emperor Constantinus 1 built a roman bath.

Italy is a country as if made for love. Watching down on the city Pontus now saw a couple in love often seen in the capital city of Rome. It was a pleasant detail, with the city of Rome, Pontus´s mother often described it. In Rome there was much time for love. It could be on the siesta, in the cafe, out in the street life, in the crowd of people, by beautiful artifacts, with the bus to the ocean in the weekend or somewhere else nice.

When Pontus had been with his mother to the silver smithy where she worked, he had seen what she was making for kind of jewelry. It was a piece of silver jewelry with a heart of silver.

It was fun to be there too. It was fun to use the iron tools. The soldering iron melted the metal down and it was warm and it was gleaming. The working tool was strange and a bit peculiar Pontus thought. The metal then could be melted down into different shapes. The contact cable head was to be brought out of the contact, otherwise there could be problems and something could catch fire in the silver smithy. It could be a piece of paper or some item made of wool. There was a special kind of smell of the gleam, when Pontus´s mother was working, leading on different kinds of heart shaped jewelry. The jewelry she would later on shape to necklaces or medallions.

This night the mother sat and thought by the kitchen table and wondered about this chore- if she had forgotten to take out the connector cord and she worried about what chores she had done before closing the door and leaving the silver smithy. Did she forget to take out the cable cord to the soldering iron? She was worried when she couldn´t manage to find out a good answer about this question. Thus she stressed up from the kitchen chair and went toward the long hall way, to take on the rain jacket, and out she went into the rain - back toward the silver smith!

Out in the rain she met the man she was living with. He was also living in this apartment with the long hall way and it was like that, that they lived there together - like other romans live together in homes and apartments. It was more or less a practical thing to live together, Pontus´s mother thought of their way of living. Some things it was good to be two about, as an adult. Even if it could be - well... difficult sometimes. The meeting between these two quickly passed in the rain slippery stone street.

-"Hello. Are you staying here tonight. I have to hurry away to work."...

The horse movements made Pontus feel very tired. He relaxed himself some and fell asleep. He fell deeper and deeper into sleep there on the horse and soon he started dreaming. Pontus was now at home on the square with his mother and friends. The horse was there too. And it was seated on the military museum roof.

It could be seen from the market place on Piazzo Navone. Pontus sat in a ring of buyers. They were having their lunch. The lunch was always good on the Piazzo Navone square on Sundays.

-"Delicious!"

There were croissants, cup cades and sausages from Vienna Hanz. He was from Vienna. Vienna is in Austria. Together they had visited the Italian country side with el Castello -the castle. The country side was nice with its green surroundings and flower gardens and the people had a relaxed way of life. The horses were fascinating! the children thought and they used to play together that they were horses on the square – that they were horses on the Italian country side. Then they felt so free! It was so nice to just be out there and run Pontus thought. Pontus thought about the food in the country side.

Then Pontus woke up. The horse had stopped. It was now standing still eating on a field. The horse had become hungry of course! It was now eating in the green grass. Pontus felt the hunger and the Aching feeling for potatoes, pistachios nuts.... Then there was a smell of greens... It was carrots! Pontus had a taste of some from a small waggon standing nearby with vegetables next to a garden.

The clouds were leave thin over the country side and the greens. The fields were plowed and there most certainly were potatoes here. Potatoes would have been so tasty now, thought Pontus, but he settled with the raw carrots. There was soil under Pontus´s feet. With his dusty fingers he took a strong take of the carrots.

-"Wheh!" but the taste of carrot was good.

The horse stood with earthy hooves in the soil as it was eating from the greens. Pontus grabbed the horse´s mane where it was and felt with his hand under the horse´s mane. It was warm and strong and the smell of horse was so good!

Coo! such wonderful feelings it was to ride this big lively horse that puffed strongly! It was so nice to be there a bit above the ground with a kind of bigger perspective from the horse´s back! All of a sudden Pontus felt how it started to hail icy snow from the sky.

The horse was snorting in dispraise and scratching the ground in dispraise, with its hooves. The horse sat off in a strong pace and then lifted up into the sky. The hail was raining down over them and it was so difficult to see from the horse. The horse flew quickly with its wings and finally it had taken them away from the hail storm.

Pontus saw his mother down on a square.

-"Mother! Shouted Pontus when he saw her from the sky. How I´ve missed you! I love you!" The horse slowed down and seemed to understand that Pontus wanted to get off the horse. The horse landed softly on the street cobble stones and they met in a warm hug!

-"Oh how happy I am to see you again Pontus! I was wondering... But oh! - What a sight! I recognize this horse Pontus, she started saying but paused herself. But we have to get into the warmth now Pontus. We´ll freeze otherwise".

They ran away from the place on the square hand in hand mother and son, home towards the warmth, hugs, fairy tales and maybe even more fantastic adventures!

They didn´t see the horse any more on that day. It flew away. The morning after it was back once more on the national museum roof.

But what happened with the soldering iron in the silver smith is another issue. They didn´t know. There might have been a fire even. If so it should have been brought out by all of the hail and the rain in the stormy weather.

THE END

WORKS CITED

Giuseppi Vicari; "Beyond conceptual dualism – Ontology of Consciousness, Mental Causation, and Holism in John R Searle´s Philosphy of Mind" Amsterdam - New York, NY 2008

Hüseyin Çimrin; "The Metropolis of antique age Ephesus" Oluşur Basim 2013

Photographs: Sandra Aastroem

Paintings: Sandra Aastroem

Illustrations: Authorhouse UK

ABOUT THE AUTHOR

Sandra Aastroem is a Swedish first time published author. Sandra Aastroem graduated in 2004 from the social worker education in the Mid Sweden University. Since then she has been working in different fields of Social Work.

Sandra Aastroem married in 2006 and has two children Vilmer and Maximilian. She lives in the small town of Fraansta, in Sweden.

INDEX

Printed in the United States
By Bookmasters